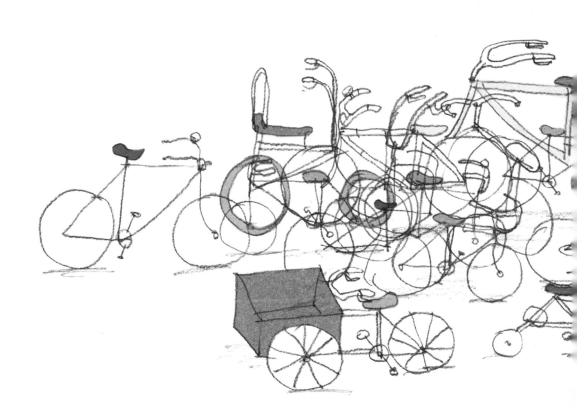

For **Elsie**

Cataloging-in-Publication Data has been applied for and may
be obtained from the Library of Congress.
ISBN: 978-1-4197-0036-1

First published in hardcover in Great Britain by
HarperCollins Children's Books in 2011
HarperCollins Children's Books is a division of
HarperCollins Publishers Ltd.

Text and illustrations copyright © David Mackintosh 2011
Book designed and lettered by David Mackintosh

Printed and bound in China
10 9 8 7 6 5 4 3 2 1

Abrams Books for Young Readers are available at special discounts when purchased
in quantity for premiums and promotions as well as fundraising or educational
use. Special editions can also be created to specification. For details, contact
specialsales@abramsbooks.com or the address below.

ABRAMS
THE ART OF BOOKS SINCE 1949
115 West 18th Street
New York, NY 10011
www.abramsbooks.com

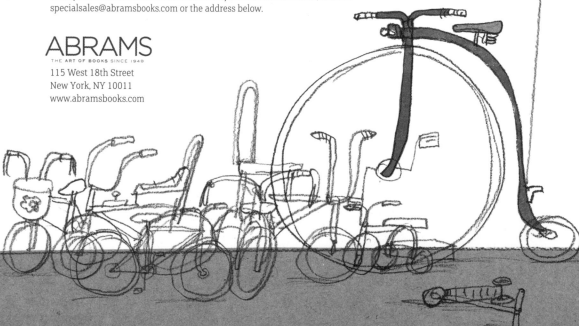

MARSHALL ARMSTRONG is NEW to OUR SCHOOL

David Mackintosh

Abrams Books for Young Readers

New York

Marshall Armstrong is new to our school.
Ms. Wright says he should sit at the front of our class,
just for the first few days until he settles in.

He looks different to me.

Marshall Armstrong sits next to me.
His things are different from mine.

Marshall Armstrong's ear
looks like a shell.

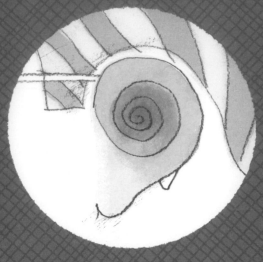

His hair reminds me of
driving in the countryside
to visit Grandma.

His glasses belong
to another boy.

His laces are straight,
not crisscrossed,
like mine.

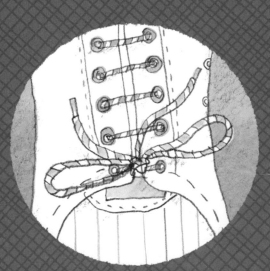

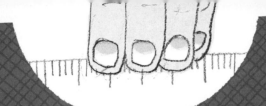

His freckles look like birdseed on his nose.

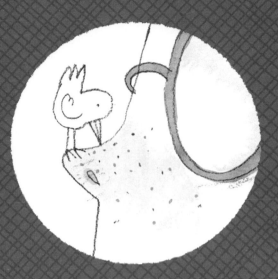

He has lips like my tropical fish, Ninja.

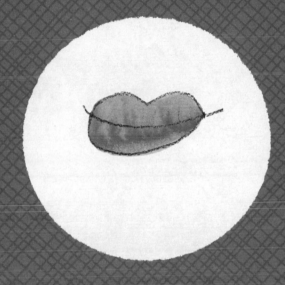

And his eyes are always   focused on Ms. Wright.

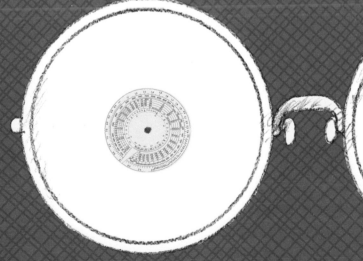

Marshall Armstrong's arm is too close to mine.

It is all white with red bumps on it.

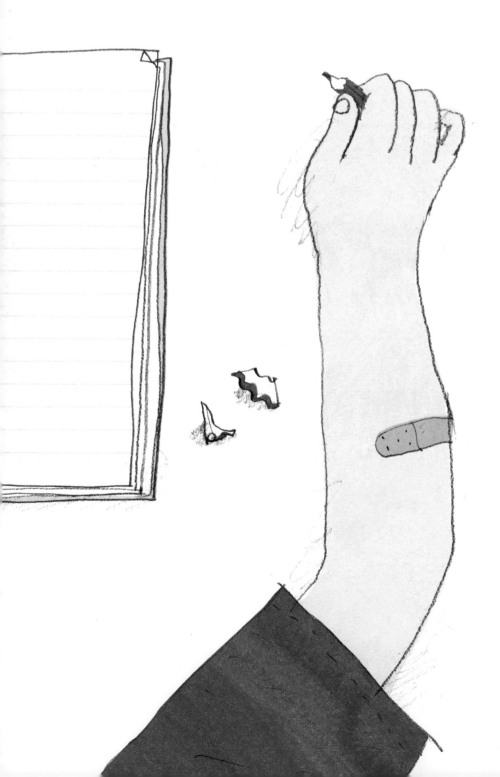

He says it's because mosquitoes like him more than me.

His watch doesn't even have hands.

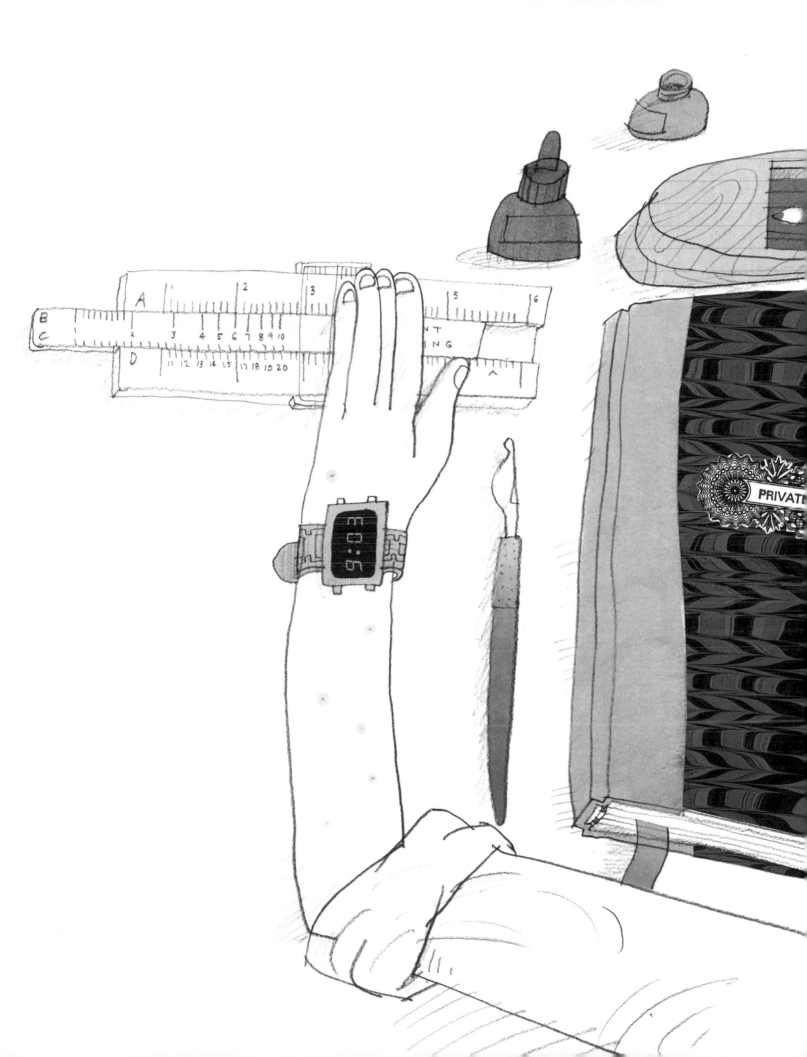

Marshall Armstrong doesn't eat normal food.
We call it "space food," because it comes in silver wrappers.
Every wrapper has the name of the food inside it
written on the outside in black letters.

Then he has
a fuzzy peach
for dessert.

Marshall Armstrong can't play at recess.
His doctor says that he should just sit with the
medicine balls and read his book.

Marshall Armstrong always wears a hat outside –
it's because of the ozone layer.

He tends to stay
in the shade.

Marshall Armstrong doesn't have a TV at home. He prefers the paper. His dad says it gives him a good perspective.

Marshall Armstrong doesn't fit in at our school.

Not one bit.

Marshall Armstrong has invited
everyone at school to his birthday party.
My mom says I have to go.

AND give him a present.

I'll probably have to sit next to him
the whole time, just like in school.

AND we won't be allowed to run around outside . . .

AND we won't eat fancy birthday cake
OR drink soda . . .

AND we'll all have to be careful
not to get too *hot and bothered* . . .

AND he'll make us read the
newspaper with his dad . . .

AND EVERYONE WILL
HAVE A TERRIBLE TIME.

Especially

ME.

BUT at
Marshall Armstrong's
house . . .

we can
run around
inside . . .

And...

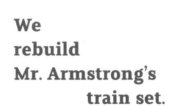

Marshall Armstrong welcomes us by playing "Happy Birthday" on the piano he and his dad made.

1, 2, 3, 4, 5, 6, 7, 8, 9, 10, 11, 12, 13, 14, 15, 16, 17, 18, 19, 20...

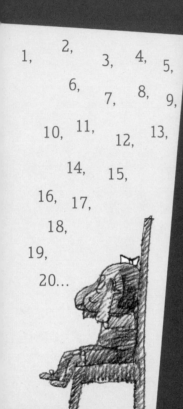

We rebuild Mr. Armstrong's train set.

We all take turns trying to light the bulb.

Jeffrey Feather wins blind man's bluff twice, without looking.

We help put up Marshall Armstrong's jungle tent.

We have organic birthday cake, hot dogs, and carrot cupcakes.

There is REAL lemonade made from lemons. And with seeds.

There is a piñata to break open.

We play hide-and-seek all over the house.

Bernadette has to go home early.

We swing on monkey bars.

Marshall Armstrong completes the obstacle course in record time.

Then Mrs. Armstrong lets us have a power nap.

We take turns looking at the sky through a telescope, and through a microscope at the cut on Jane's arm.

Marshall Armstrong performs on the piano he and his dad made, and he shows us a game with long wooden sticks called "cues."

OBSERVATORY ACCESS ONLY.

Then,

we all
ride down
the special
fireman's pole,
from the top
of the house to
the bottom.

Mr. Armstrong
says that it's
in case of
emergencies,
but you can also
use it if you're
in a hurry to
answer the
front door . . .

URSUS
ARCTOS
HORRIBILIS

or go to the bathroom.

Before we leave, Marshall Armstrong's mother gives each of us a party bag with our name on it.

I get Monster Gripping Paws, itching powder, and blood capsules. And a key ring with a light on it, which I save for my mom.

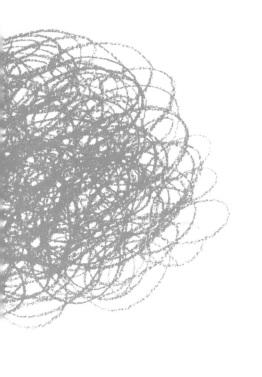

I tell her,

We had a GREAT time at
Marshall Armstrong's party.

And Marshall is great too.

Elizabeth Bell is new to our school.
I tell Ms. Wright that she should sit at the front
with me and Marshall for the first few days,
until she settles in.